PENCASTER ➡

This Postman Pat Special Delivery Service Annual belongs to

....

Age ....

EGMONT
We bring stories to life

First published in Great Britain in 2010
by Egmont UK Limited
239 Kensington High Street, London W8 6SA
Text by Laura Green • Designed by Anthony Duke

ISBN 978 1 4052 5369 7
1 3 5 7 9 10 8 6 4 2
Printed in Italy

Contents

SDS Helicopter

SDS Small

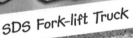
SDS Fork-lift Truck

SDS Large Van

SDS Motorbike

Welcome!

Postman Pat in his van

Forge Cottage

Pat Clifton lives in Forge Cottage. He is Greendale and Pencaster's top postman!

Postman Pat's black and white cat, **Jess** loves to discover things. This can lead to lots of adventures with Postman Pat!

Julian Clifton loves playing football and going to Pencaster United matches with his dad. His favourite superhero is Captain Zapp!

Sara Clifton is Postman Pat's wife. She works in the Station Café and makes yummy cakes.

Station Café

Come and meet Postman Pat's friends!

Alf and Dorothy

Mrs Goggins sorts out the mail at the Post Office. Watch out for her little white dog, Bonnie!

Alf and Dorothy Thompson live on a small farm with their son, Bill Thompson. They have lots of sheep and grow their own vegetables.

Mrs Goggins and Bonnie

PC Selby and Lucy

Ted Glen is a handyman. He loves inventing machines, even if they don't always work out as he had planned!

PC Arthur Selby is the Greendale policeman. He makes sure the roads are safe, but often gets caught up in Postman Pat's deliveries! His daughter, Lucy Selby is very popular at Greendale School.

Ted Glen

Michael Lam

Michael Lam runs the mobile shop. He is also a talented chef and loves making surprise recipes for his friends.

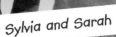
Sylvia and Sarah

Reverend Timms is the Greendale vicar. He likes to play the banjo and rock'n'roll on the church piano!

Reverend Timms

Dr Sylvia Gilbertson works at the clinic in Greendale. **Sarah Gilbertson** is her daughter. Sarah loves to talk and talk and talk!

Amy and Pumpkin

The Greendale vet is **Amy Wrigglesworth**. She drives a 4x4 and has a naughty pony called **Pumpkin**.

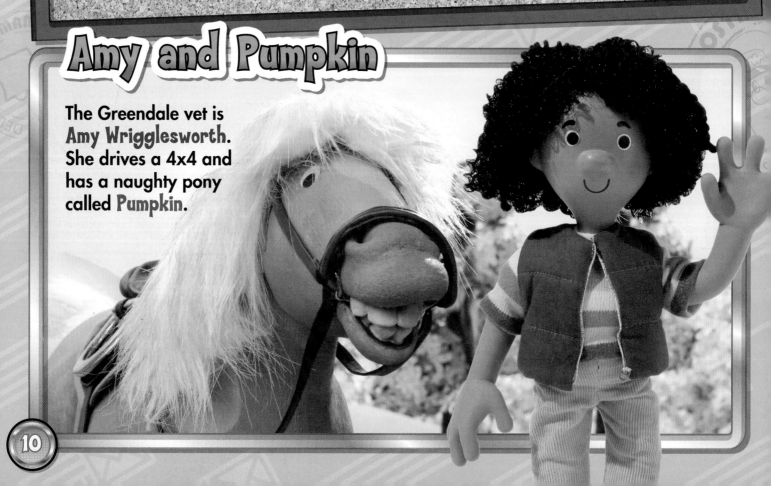

Meet the Bains Family

Ajay Bains drives the Pencaster Flyer. Sometimes Ajay gets into trouble on the tracks . . . find out more about that later on!

Nisha Bains works hard running the Station Café.

Pencaster Flyer

Meera and Nikhil are brother and sister. Meera loves snowboarding, playing pirates and making ice cream. Nikhil likes to throw food around!

Ben Taylor

Lauren and Lizzy Taylor

Ben Taylor is the general manager of the Pencaster Mail Centre. He helps Postman Pat sort his deliveries. Ben's wife, Lauren is a teacher at Greendale School. Their daughter Lizzy loves to do wheelies and play out with her friends!

WHEEEEE!

Special Delivery Service Vehicles

It is very important that Postman Pat chooses the right vehicle for each delivery. Come and see some of the Special Delivery Service vehicles!

Special Delivery Service MOTORBIKE

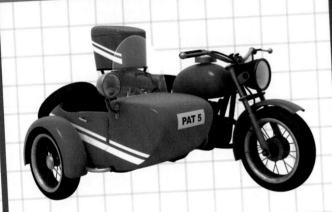

Perfect for a small parcel that needs to be delivered fast! There's a sidecar for Jess, too!

Special Delivery Service SMALL VAN

This van is great if Postman Pat has lots of small parcels and letters to deliver.

Here's Postman Pat finding a short cut!

Here's Postman Pat dropping off a parcel at Ted's garage!

Which is your favourite?

Special Delivery Service
HELICOPTER

When the delivery is too big for the van, Postman Pat hops into his flying machine!

Special Delivery Service
LARGE VAN

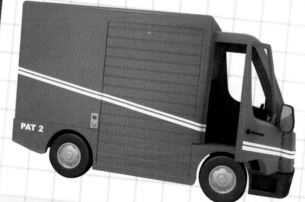

This van has got an automatic ramp so Postman Pat can get heavy parcels into the back in no time.

Here's Postman Pat delivering a runaway cow!

Here's Postman Pat zooming through the country lanes!

Speedy Car

Julian Clifton was excited. That afternoon he was going to Bill Thompson's birthday party. It was fancy dress and Julian had dressed up as a cowboy!

"As you look like such a hero, you can help me with my deliveries before the party," said Postman Pat.
"Let's get to work, cowboy!"

YEE-HAAA!

Postman Pat and Julian raced over to the Mail Centre. Ben had three special deliveries waiting for them.

"I've got two presents for Bill. You need to deliver them to Greendale Café for the party," said Ben. "And this parcel is for Ted at the garage. Ted needs it right away."

"No problem!" said Postman Pat. "You can count on us!"

When Postman Pat and Julian arrived at Ted's garage, it was full of smoke!

"Don't worry, it's just a fuse," said Ted. "I'm fixing Mrs Goggins's television. I just need my new remote control. Have you got the parcel?"

Julian handed Ted one of the parcels.

"Now that's what I call a remote!" said Ted. "Thanks, cowboy!"

Postman Pat, Julian and Jess set off for the party. They hadn't gone far when they heard a strange rumbling noise in the back of the van.

Postman Pat opened the van door. A little yellow car jumped out and sped off down the lane!

"That's Bill's present," gasped Julian. "It's getting away!"

BRRUUUMM! BRRUUUUUMMMM!

WOAH!

Back at the garage, Ted was trying to use his new remote control.

"It seems to be broken," he said, pressing the buttons. The television stayed blank. "What's going on?"

Meanwhile, Postman Pat, Julian and Jess were chasing the runaway car all over Pencaster. Everytime the car came to a stop, it whizzed back into action again!

"Come on, Dad!" puffed Julian. "We've got to catch it!"

Suddenly, the car screeched to a stop in Alf Thompson's field.

As Postman Past went to grab it, the car started up again and zoomed through Julian's legs. Julian, Postman Pat and Jess fell on to the ground with a big **BUMP!**

"It's getting away again!" said Julian.

Then Postman Pat had an idea. He ran to the back of the van and opened the third parcel.

"We can stop the car with the control!" said Postman Pat. But before he had a chance to press the button, the car stopped by itself.

"Huh?" Postman Pat said, pressing the buttons on the remote control. Nothing happened. "Hmm … it doesn't seem to work."

Then he had a thought. "Aha! Ted must have the control for the car and we've got Ted's TV remote control. Ted is controlling the car!"

OH NO!

"I gave Ted the wrong parcel!" Julian gasped.

"The Special Delivery Service never gives up, Julian," replied Postman Pat. "Hop in the van. We need to find Ted before the party starts."

When they arrived at Ted's garage, Mrs Goggins and her dog, Bonnie, were outside. The runaway car leaped out of the back of the van and crashed into Bonnie.

"Bonnie!" yelled Mrs Goggins, as the car zoomed out of the garage with Bonnie riding on top!

"We'll get her back!" said Postman Pat. He turned to Julian. "Come on cowboy, we've got a dog to rescue!"

Postman Pat and Julian set off, chasing the runaway car.

"We're not going to make it!" said Julian. "The party starts in ten minutes!"

Just then, Julian heard a loud siren. It was PC Selby.

"This is a job for an officer of the law," PC Selby said, joining in the chase.

The car came to a stop at the edge of the cliff.

"It's too dangerous to reach it," warned PC Selby.

"But Bill isn't going to get his present!" said Julian.

"Oh yes he is!" Postman Pat replied. "Have you still got your lasso, Julian?"

Suddenly, they all froze. The car and Bonnie were heading for the cliff!

Postman Pat jumped out of his van. He threw a stick into the air and Bonnie jumped up from the car to catch it.

"Phew! Well done, Pat!" PC Selby said. "One dog rescued!"

Yee ha!

"Here goes!" said Postman Pat, and he swung the lasso at the car. It wrapped around the wheels!

With one big pull, Postman Pat dragged the car towards him.

"Hurrah!" cried Julian.

"Let's get this delivery back on the road!" said Postman Pat.

Postman Pat, Julian and Jess zoomed over to the café just as Bill's party was starting. Bill was so happy when he saw his remote-control car!

"Wow!" said Bill. "This is the best present ever!"

"All in a day's work for the Special Delivery Service," said Postman Pat. "Mission accomplished!"

ON THE MOVE!

Draw a wiggly line between the person and the vehicle he drives. When you've finished, draw a circle around the vehicle you would most like to go for a ride in!

1

2

3

4

a

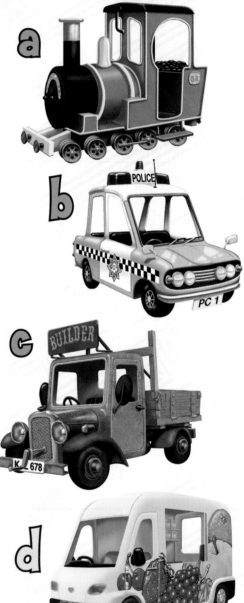

b

POLICE

PC 1

c

BUILDER

KL 678

d

MXL94

Answers on page 68.

NAME SEARCH

Can you find the names in the word grid? They can read across or down. There is one name that is not in the grid. When you know which one, shout out the missing name!

Ajay ☐   Jess ☐

Amy ☐   Julian ☐

Meera ☐   Lauren ☐

Ben ☐

a	m	e	e	r	a	e	b
s	o	p	c	w	r	h	a
n	j	u	l	i	a	n	j
b	i	q	a	l	m	e	a
e	r	s	u	g	y	g	y
n	e	c	r	r	e	k	l
b	f	v	e	j	b	q	h
o	p	b	n	a	n	s	d

Answers on page 68.

HOLD ON TIGHT!

There's been a storm in Greendale. Can you guide Postman Pat and Jess back to Forge Cottage? Watch out for the fallen trees – they are blocking some of the routes!

START

FINISH

How many fallen trees can you see?

Answers on page 68.

COLOUR TIME

Ted Glen is trying out his new invention. Add colour to the scene to bring his paint-mixing machine to life.

POSTCARD HOME

PC Selby and Lucy Selby have gone on holiday. Read Lucy's postcard to her classmates, then draw a picture for the front of the postcard below.

Hello, everyone!

We are having the best holiday ever! It has been snowing every day so we are wrapped up in scarves and hats. Yesterday we went skiing down a snowy mountain. It was so cool!

See you all soon,
Lucy x

MRS TAYLOR'S CLASS

GREENDALE SCHOOL

GREENDALE

BALLOON BONANZA

Julian is on his way to a party but all of his balloons have blown away! Count how many balloons you can see. Every time you see one, shout 'balloon'!

I can count [ ] balloons!

SUPER MAGNET

Postman Pat had arrived at the Mail Centre to pick up a special delivery. A giant magnet!

"A water tower has fallen on the train track in Greendale," Ben told Postman Pat. "The magnet is the only thing that can pick it up."

"Oh dear," said Postman Pat. "We'd better get moving, Jess!"

Over in Greendale, Ted and Ajay were waiting for Postman Pat. The Pencaster Flyer was stuck. Ajay couldn't get it past the water tower.

"I'll attach the magnet to this crane, the tower will stick to the magnet, we'll lift the tower off the track, and bish bash bosh, you can get your train through!" said Ted.

"Let's just hope Pat gets here quickly," replied Ajay, glancing at his watch.

Back at the Mail Centre, Ben was showing Postman Pat the remote control for the magnet.

"Whatever you do, don't turn it ..." began Ben.

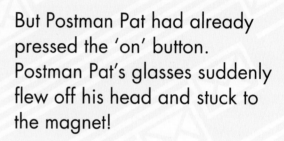

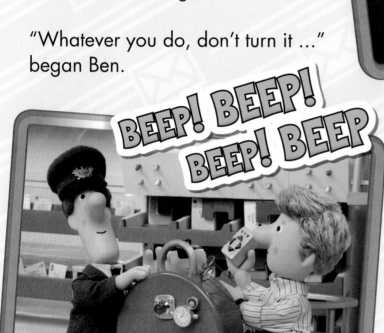

BEEP! BEEP! BEEP! BEEP

But Postman Pat had already pressed the 'on' button. Postman Pat's glasses suddenly flew off his head and stuck to the magnet!

Then the metal tag on Jess's collar sprung up. Jess slid across the floor towards the magnet! Ben's arm flew out as the magnet pulled his watch.

"Woah! I see what you mean!" said Postman Pat, turning off the remote control. "I'll be careful next time."

Ben quickly attached the magnet to the helicopter and Postman Pat set off for Greendale.

"Special Delivery Service! Permission to land!" Pat shouted down, as he approached the water tower.

"Pat's here! Right, I'll reverse the train back to the station," said Ajay, jumping into his cabin. "Ted, when I hear your signal, I'll set off from Greendale."

OH NO!

BEEP! BEEP!

Ajay reversed the train while Postman Pat got ready to land. But the helicopter started to shake. The remote control crashed onto the cockpit floor. The 'on' button started to flash!

"Oh no, not again!" cried Postman Pat.

The magnet stuck to the moving train.

"I can't reach the control!" Postman Pat cried, as the train pulled them through the countryside.

Jess nudged the control towards Postman Pat's feet, and he finally turned it off. The helicopter shot back up into the sky.

"Oh dear, now we're miles away!" Postman Pat said. "Let's head back to find Ted."

But Postman Pat didn't notice that the remote control was flashing again. The magnet had switched itself back on!

As Postman Pat flew over Greendale, the magnet was causing all sorts of trouble. It ripped a weather vane off the church roof.

Then it pulled PC Selby's helmet from his head!

"Come back with that!" cried PC Selby.

Postman Pat and Jess didn't notice a thing.

At Greendale Farm, Amy was grooming Pumpkin, when her bridle suddenly flew upwards.

"Huh? What's going on?" cried Amy, as the bridle zipped up into the sky!

Meanwhile, Ted was still waiting by the water tower. "Where on earth is Pat?" he said. "Ajay's waiting for me to pull the lever."

Just then, Postman Pat flew over Ted's head. The force of the magnet pulled the metal lever forward!

29

Over at Greendale Station, the lever triggered the signal bell. **Ding! Ding! Ding!**

"Ah, they must have cleared the track," Ajay said, starting up the train. "It's time to go!"

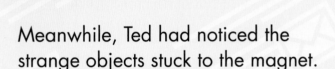

Meanwhile, Ted had noticed the strange objects stuck to the magnet.

"Oh dear," said Postman Pat. "The magnet must have come on again!"

Postman Pat quickly turned the magnet back off. The objects dropped to the ground just as PC Selby, Amy and Alf ran on to the platform.

"What's going on 'ere then?" PC Selby asked, picking up his hat. "Somebody stole my ..."

"I'll explain later," Postman Pat called down. "Let's get this water tower shifted and fast!"

Suddenly, Postman Pat heard a familiar noise. **Ding! Ding! Ding!** It was the train signal. The Pencaster Flyer was on its way!

DING! DING!

"We don't have time to attach the magnet to the crane!" said Ted. "Can you lift the tower with your helicopter, Pat?"

"I'll do my best, Ted!" Postman Pat called down.

Postman Pat switched the magnet on.

"You've got to be quick, Pat," Ted called up. "The train is coming!"

Postman Pat got the helicopter into position. The magnet stuck to the water tower. But when Pat tried to lift it, he couldn't lift it high enough.

"It's too heavy!" Postman Pat shouted down.

"Keep trying!" Ted said.

Postman Pat moved his helicopter lower and flew back up quickly. This time, the magnet picked up the water tower. Postman Pat lifted it off the tracks.

"You did it, Pat!" said Ted, just as the Pencaster Flyer zoomed by!

"Well done!" said PC Selby.

"That was a close one!" Postman Pat said. "Special Delivery Service – mission accomplished!"

Mission accomplished!

31

MEMORY QUIZ

Now you have read Super Magnet, can you remember what happened? It's time to find out! Take the quiz below by ticking the correct answers.

1. What vehicle did Pat use to deliver the magnet?

motorbike ☐

helicopter ☐

big van ☐

2. Who lost their horse bridle?

PC Selby ☐

Ted ☐

Amy ☐

3. The magnet was controlled by a remote control.

TRUE ☐   FALSE ☐

4. Who was driving the Pencaster Flyer?

Ajay

Jess

Mrs Goggins

5. What did the magnet steal from PC Selby's Head?

glasses

helmet

cake

6. What was blocking the train track?

parcel

Pumpkin

water tower

How many did you remember?

Answers on page 68.

WHAT GOES WHERE?

Match the things below to the different places around Greendale and Pencaster.

1. Fork-lift Truck

2. Spanner

3. Sheep

4. Pencaster Flyer

a) Greendale Hills

b) Pencaster Station

c) Mail Centre

d) Ted's Garage

Answers on page 68.

FIND THE OBJECTS!

Woah! Postman Pat is about to drop an egg!
Can you find the 5 objects in the main picture before the
egg cracks on the floor? Tick the objects as you find them.

Answers on page 68.

MEMORY GAME

Look at this photograph carefully for a few minutes.
Then cover it up and see if you can answer the questions.
Say the answers out loud!

1. What tool is Ted holding?

2. Is Jess in the photograph?

3. What colour is the toolbox?

4. Is the sky blue or grey?

5. Has PC Selby got a hat on?

SNOWY PUZZLE

It's time for a snowball fight! Can you work out who's hiding behind the snowballs? Shout their names out when you know.

1

2

3

4

A snowy Christmas in Greendale

Answers on page 68.

DELIVERY GAME

You have your own delivery to make. You need to take a pair of robots to Pencaster train station! You can play this game with a friend. You will need a die and a counter each. The first one to make it to the station wins the gold star award. Good luck!

START

The robots spill a bag of letters. Go back to the start.

Take a boat across the lake.

The robots knock over Mrs Goggins' milk! Go back 2 places.

Get the robots into the van. Go forward 2 places.

Race through Pencaster Square. Go forward 2 places.

Zoom past Ted's garage. Go forward 1 place.

17   18

Alf Thompson's sheep have blocked the road! Go back 2 places.

PC Selby closes the bridge! Go back 2 places.

20

Oh no! You skid down a muddy lane.

21

15

22

23

14

Pick up the Special Delivery Service helicopter! Go forward 4 places.

25

26

FINISH

MISSION ACCOMPLISHED!

You can't land the helicopter at the train station. Go back 5 places.

28   29   30

SDS AWARD ★★★

DISCO MACHINE

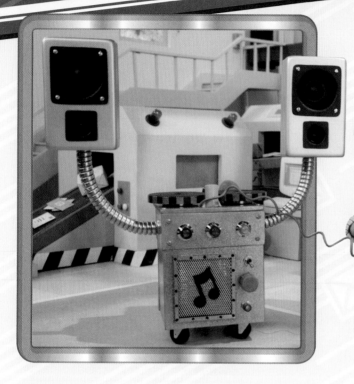

Postman Pat has just arrived at the Mail Centre to pick up a disco machine.

"You need to deliver it to Greendale School. Woo hoo hoo," Ben sang into the microphone. "The children are having a disco."

"Ooh, that sounds like fun!" smiled Postman Pat, loading the machine on to the fork-lift truck.

"This will be no problem for the Special Delivery Serv ..." Postman Pat began. Suddenly the truck whizzed forward. Postman Pat crashed into the railing!

Wires popped out of one of the speakers.

"Uh oh! There's only one man who can fix this," said Postman Pat. "Ben, can you call Ted Glen and tell him I'm on my way?"

CRASH!

BANG! BANG! BANG!

At Ted's garage ...

"Don't you worry, Pat," said Ted, taking out his hammer. "I'll have this fixed in no time."

"Erm, Ted. Be careful ..." said Postman Pat, frowning.

Over at Greendale School, Amy and Lauren were getting everything ready for the disco.

"The kids are going to love the disco machine," Lauren said. "Pat will be here soon!"

Back at the garage, Ted had just finished fixing the disco machine.

"It's as good as new!" said Postman Pat.

"It's even better than that," replied Ted.

Ted pressed a button. Sparkly bubbles poured out of the machine!

"Right, Jess. Let's get this bubbly delivery back on the road!" said Postman Pat.

But Postman Pat and Jess hadn't got very far before they hit another problem.

PC Selby had closed the bridge into Greendale.

"Sorry, Pat," said PC Selby. "You can't come across here today. It is closed for repairs."

"Oh dear!" gasped Postman Pat. "But it's the only way into Greendale!"

Back at the school, the children had arrived for the disco, but there was no sign of the disco machine.

"It's not much of a disco without music," frowned Bill.

"My dad will get here," replied Julian. "I just know it."

Meanwhile, Postman Pat was still stuck in Pencaster.
"If I can't get into Greendale by road, there's
only one other way ... the helicopter!"

Postman Pat sped back to the mail centre.

"Ben, I need you to get the helicopter
ready," said Postman Pat
"This delivery needs to
hit the sky!"

"No problem, Pat,"
Ben replied.

The helicopter was
ready in record time.
Postman Pat and Jess
jumped on board.

"Fly safely," Ben
called up.

"Thanks, Ben!" said
Postman Pat. "Hold
on tight, Jess!"

The helicopter whizzed up into the sky.
As they zoomed over the rooftops, the disco
machine switched itself on. Hundreds of little
bubbles floated down on Pencaster!

"Just look at that, Jess!" smiled Postman Pat.

Back at the school, everyone was getting worried. Then they heard a loud chugging noise outside. Postman Pat had arrived!

"Hurrah!" the children chorused.

"I knew you'd make it, Dad!" said Julian, happily.

Postman Pat switched on the disco machine. Music boomed out of the speakers and the room filled up with bubbles.

"This is the best disco in the world!" said Bill.

"I think it's time for me to have a boogie, too" said Postman Pat. "Special Delivery Service — mission accomplished."

"Bubble-tastic!"

LET'S BOOGIE

Everyone in Greendale is having a dance!
Circle the odd one out in each row.

 a
 b
 c
 d

a
b
c
d

a
b
c
d

a
b
c
d

Answers on page 68.

MUSIC FROM MARS

I'm planning my own Greendale disco. The theme is outer space. Draw a picture for my poster!

TED GLEN'S JIVE FROM OUTER SPACE!

5PM AT THE TOWN SQUARE
FANCY DRESS: ALIENS, ROBOTS, ROCKETS!

JUMBLED UP

This picture is all mixed up! Can you work out who it is?

Write his name below. Can you tell where he is?

_____ __ _____

Answers on page 68.

SPOT THE DIFFERENCE

Charlie, Julian, Bill and Sarah have dressed up as superheroes for the day!

These two pictures look the same but 5 things are different in picture 2. Circle the differences and tick the boxes as you find each one.

1 2 3 4 5

2

WHAT TIME IS IT?

We're very busy, and always on the go! Read the time on the clocks to help us get to our jobs on time.

1. It's early in the morning. Postman Pat has to go to the Mail Centre to collect his deliveries. What time does he have to go?

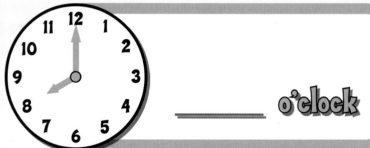

_____ o'clock

2. The first delivery of the day is for Alf Thompson at Thompson Ground. What time does Alf need his delivery?

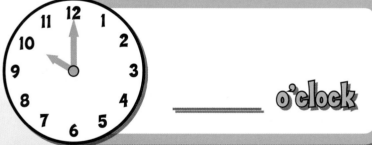

_____ o'clock

3. Mrs Goggins has made a delicious lunch for Postman Pat and Julian. She gives Jess a big bowl of fish, too! What time is lunch?

_____ o'clock

4. Postman Pat has got a special delivery for Amy – a new bridle for Pumpkin. What time does Postman Pat have to be at the surgery?

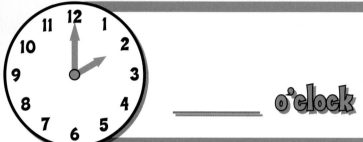

_____ o'clock

5. An urgent delivery is arriving on the Pencaster Flyer. Let's hope Postman Pat makes it to Pencaster Station in time! What time does the train arrive?

_____ o'clock

6. It's nearly home time! Postman Pat has one last thing to do. He needs to pick up a cake for his tea. What time does Mrs Goggins' shop close?

_____ o'clock

A Surprise Party

At the mail centre, Ben, Sarah and Julian were planning a surprise party for Postman Pat. They were going to present him with a Special Delivery Gold Star!

"We only award the Gold Star to the very best postmen," said Ben.

"Wow!" said Julian, hanging up the decorations. "Dad's going to get such a surprise!"

Over in Greendale, Postman Pat had just arrived at the Post Office to pick up a special delivery.

"Ben wants you to take it to the Mail Centre by 2 o'clock," said Mrs Goggins.

"We haven't got long, Jess," Postman Pat replied. "We'd better hit the road!"

Back at the Mail Centre, Nisha had arrived with cakes and more decorations. There were a lot of boxes!

"We're never going to get the party ready for 2 o'clock," frowned Ben.

Ben looked at his computer to check on Postman Pat. "Pat's heading towards Alf Thompson's Ground," he said, picking up his mobile phone. "Let's see if Alf can hold him there for a bit."

Alf answered his phone straight away.

"Stall Pat, you say?" Alf said to Ben. "You leave it to me!"

Alf tipped up his truck, spilling hay bales all over the road. "Let's see Pat get past this lot!" he chuckled.

Postman Pat soon pulled up in his van. "What's happened here?" he asked. "I've got a special delivery to make!"

"Sorry, Pat," said Alf. "You won't get your delivery through here."

"Hmm ... " Postman Pat went to the back of his van. Seconds later, he zoomed down the ramp on his motorbike!

"Bye!" waved Postman Pat.

Back at the mail centre, the computer was flashing.

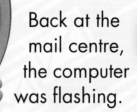

"Pat's got past Alf!" said Ben. He looked at his watch. "We've got to stop him. I'll try PC Selby."

PC Selby was happy to help. He quickly blocked off the bridge into Pencaster.

"Sorry, Pat. This bridge is closed," said PC Selby.

Postman Pat wasn't going to let a blocked bridge stop his delivery from getting through. He put two wooden planks over the river and drove right across them!

"See you later, Arthur!" smiled Postman Pat.

"Oh dear," said PC Selby into his phone. "Ben, Pat's on his way!"

Over at Pencaster Square, Ted Glen had heard the news about the surprise party.

"I bet I can stop Pat!" thought Ted. He poured a big pile of sand onto the road.

Just then, Postman Pat raced around the corner. "Ah, nearly there now, Jess!"

Postman Pat saw the big pile of sand but he couldn't stop in time. "Woah!" he cried, as he leaped over the sand, clutching the delivery in his hands!

THUD!

"We did it!" said Postman Pat, landing safely. "Nothing gets in the way of the Special Delivery Service!"

Postman Pat and Jess finally arrived at the Mail Centre. Postman Pat flung open the door.

"Phew, that was a hard delivery ..." Postman Pat began.

"We'd like to award you with the Special Delivery Gold Star," said Ben. "For getting your deliveries through on time, every time!"

Postman Pat gasped. "Well, I almost didn't get through today!" he said.

"Yes, sorry about that!" chuckled Alf.

"Your delivery is for you, too," said Ben.

Postman opened the parcel. It was a Special Delivery Service cake! Everyone cheered.

"Special Delivery Service – mission accomplished!" said Postman Pat, proudly.

YOUR SURPRISE!

What would your best surprise present be?
Draw it inside the parcel. Don't forget to write your name on the tag
so Postman Pat knows who to deliver it to!

URGENT DELIVERY

The roads are closed and Postman Pat needs to deliver this huge bouncy castle! Which vehicle would you choose to make the delivery?

The bouncy castle!

small van ☐

helicopter ☐

motorbike ☐

Answer on page 68.

COLOURING QUIZ

Look at this picture, then answer these questions about it.

1. What is Jess trying to catch?

a butterfly ☐   a bird ☐   a bat ☐   Can you draw one more?

2. How many flowers can you count? Circle the number.

1   2   3   4   5   6   7   8

3. What is PC Selby riding on?

a skateboard ☐   a surfboard ☐   a bicycle ☐

4. How many clouds can you count?

There are ☐ clouds.   Now draw some more!

Now colour in the picture!

5. Is there a sun in the sky?

yes ☐   no ☐   If not, draw a big yellow sun!

Answers on page 68.

CHRISTMAS STOCKING

It was Christmas Eve in Pencaster. That evening a special Christmas party was taking place in the Town Square.

"The children are going to love it!" said Sara, putting the star on top of the tree.

Meanwhile, Postman Pat was busy taking a giant stocking over to Greendale School.

The children were going to fill it with surprise presents for the grown-ups!

The children were all very excited when they saw Postman Pat land the helicopter in the playground!

"Okay, kids ... grab your presents!" said Lauren. "One at a time!"

When all of the presents were safely inside the stocking, Postman Pat hopped back into the helicopter. Next stop, the Town Square!

RRIIIPPP!

But as Postman Pat flew over Greendale, something terrible happened ... the stocking ripped open!

BUMP!

One by one, presents tumbled through the sky.

BUMP! One landed right in the middle of Alf Thompson's field. The cows got quite a shock!

Postman Pat and Jess didn't notice a thing.

As Postman Pat flew back over the Mail Centre, Ben was waving to Pat from below.

"Pat, the presents have disappeared! There's a hole in the stocking!" he cried.

"Oh dear!" said Postman Pat, lowering the helicopter. "I'll have to go back and find them."

Ben quickly sewed the stocking together.

"That should do the trick," said Ben.

"I just hope I can find the presents in time," frowned Postman Pat, jumping back into the helicopter.

At the school, Lauren had dressed up as Father Christmas!

"The presents will be at the party by now," Lauren told the children.

The children all cheered! Everybody was very excited.

Meanwhile, Postman Pat was flying over Greendale, looking for the presents.

Jess let out a loud **MIAOOW!** Postman Pat looked down. There was a red and green present in Alf Thompson's field.

"Well done, Jess!" Postman Pat said. "Get ready to land!"

Amy Wrigglesworth was busy grooming Pumpkin when Postman Pat landed.

"Hi, Amy," said Postman Pat. "I'm looking for presents. They fell out of my stocking!"

"I wondered what they were doing here," Amy laughed, and handed Postman Pat two colourful presents. "I thought it was raining presents!"

Amy helped Postman Pat search for the rest of presents. By the time they were finished, it had started to snow.

"Oh dear, I can't fly the helicopter in the snow," frowned Postman Pat.

"Let's put the presents in Pumpkin's trailer," Amy said. "She can pull them to Pencaster."

"Great idea!" smile Postman Pat. "Let's hope we make it to the square before the children."

Postman Pat and Amy hadn't got far when they heard a loud **beep**. It was the school bus.

"Pat! Amy!" Lauren shouted. "We're stuck in a ditch ..." Lauren stopped when she saw the stocking. "Huh?"

"Long story," said Postman Pat. "Let's get this bus moving."

"It's too heavy to push," frowned Lauren.

"Hmm ... I think I know just the thing," said Postman Pat.

He quickly strapped Pumpkin to the front of the bus. Pumpkin pulled and pulled until the bus jumped forward. The children all cheered!

"It worked!" Postman Pat said, happily. "Right, everyone, back on the bus. We've got a special delivery to make!"

At Pencaster Square, everybody was waiting for the children.

Suddenly, a tinkling sound rang out across the square. Postman Pat, Pumpkin and the children had arrived. And Postman Pat was dressed up as Father Christmas!

"What's in the stocking, kids?" asked Ajay.

"Secret Santa presents!" replied the children, excitedly. "We made them for you grown-ups."

The grown-ups were very happy and surprised!

"This one's for you, Dad," said Julian.

It was a picture of Jess!

"This is one of the best presents I've ever had," smiled Postman Pat. "Special Delivery Service – mission accomplished!"

Happy Christmas, everyone!

ANSWERS

Page 20:
1 = c, 2 = d, 3 = b, 4 = a.

Page 21:
Jess is missing from the grid.

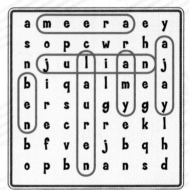

Page 22:
There are 7 fallen trees.

Page 25:
There are 8 balloons.

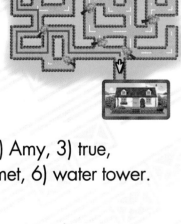

Page 32:
1) helicopter, 2) Amy, 3) true,
4) Ajay, 5) helmet, 6) water tower.

Page 34:
1) Mail Centre, 2) Ted's Garage,
3) Greendale Hills, 4) Pencaster Station.

Page 35:

Page 37:
1) Jess, 2) Julian, 3) Ben, 4) Alf.

Page 45:
Charlie = c, Jess = a, Ben = d,
Michael = b.

Page 47:
Ajay. He is at Pencaster Train Station.

Page 48:

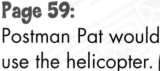

Page 59:
Postman Pat would use the helicopter.

Page 60:
1) a butterfly
2) 8 flowers
3) a bicycle
4) 3 clouds
5) no

CPSIA information can be obtained
at www.ICGtesting.com
Printed in the USA
LVRC021638041120
670703LV00014B/56